AF583360

For Sachin & Darian
— Angela

For my sister, Anna
— Ross

Written by Angela Walker
Illustrated by Ross Hamilton

Max lived next door to a big, empty house.
He longed for someone to move in. Someone he could play with.
Someone just like him.

Then one day Jun and his family arrived from Japan.

Max took Jun out to explore the neighbourhood.
They found a fluffy, fat feather lying on the ground.
Jun swished it across Max's nose.

'That tickles,' laughed Max.
Then his face began to crumple.

Max sneezed into his elbow. 'AH-CHOO!'
Jun's eyes grew wide.

Max grabbed the feather and
tickled Jun's nose.
Jun's eyes began to flutter.
Then he sneezed into his elbow.

'HAKUSHON!'
Now it was Max's turn to look surprised.

The next day Max went to the playground in search of someone else to play with.

Fleur was queuing for the flying fox. He tickled her face with his fluffy, fat feather.

Fleur's nose twitched, then her eyes closed.

'ATCHOUM!' she sneezed into her elbow.
That wasn't AH-CHOO, Max thought.
He looked around for someone else to play with.
Someone just like him.

He spied Misha by the roundabout.
Perhaps they could be friends.
He tickled Misha's nose with his fluffy, fat feather.
Misha jerked his head to one side.

'APCHKHI!' he sneezed into his elbow.

Apchkhi? Max began to wonder how many different ways there were to sneeze. He darted off to look for someone else to play with. Someone just like him.

Koa was dropping down from the monkey bars.
Max ran over and tickled his nose with his fluffy, fat feather.
Koa screwed up his eyes.

'TIHEI!' he sneezed into his elbow.
Tihei? That's different again, Max thought.

Next, he found Laura at the nest swing.
He tickled her nose with his fluffy, fat feather.
Her face scrunched into a ball.

'ATSJO!' she sneezed into her elbow.
Max sighed. This was harder than he'd expected.
He looked around for someone else.

Pri was reading by the swings.
Max tickled Pri's nose with his fluffy, fat feather.
Pri gulped in a mouthful of air.

'HACH!' she sneezed into her elbow.
Max was beginning to wonder if there was anyone left in the world just like him.

Nearby, Anja had just whizzed down the swirly slide.
Max tickled her face with his fluffy, fat feather.
Her nose began to tingle.

HATSCHI!

'HATSCHI!' she sneezed into her elbow. *Hatschi?* Max rolled the word around inside his mouth.

All he'd wanted was someone to play with. Someone just like him.

But Fleur from France said

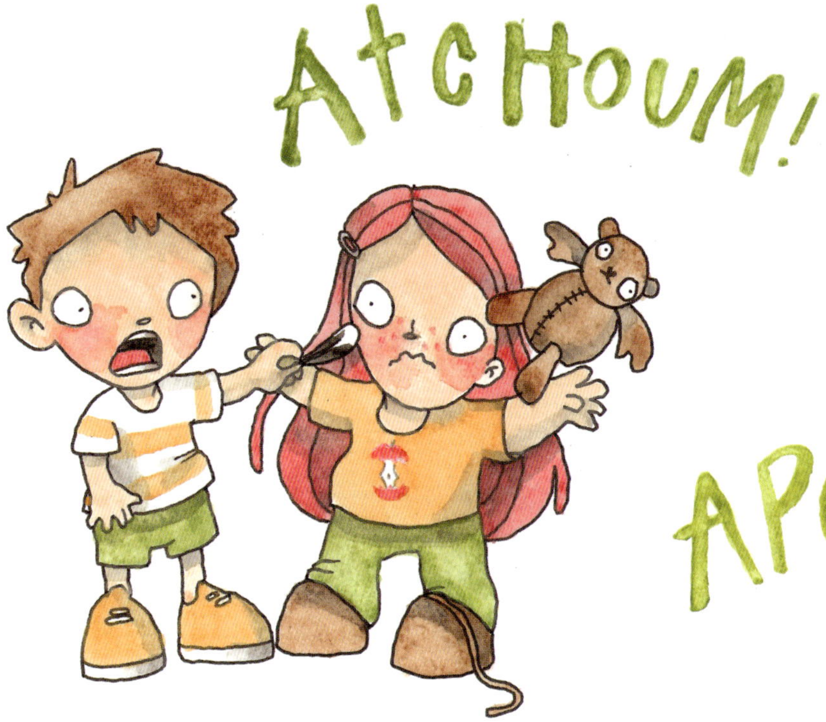

ATCHOUM!

And Misha from Russia said

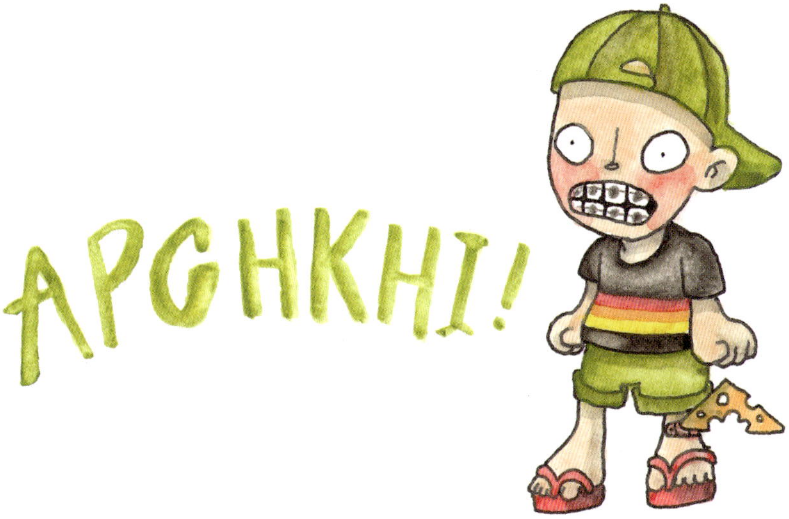

APGHKHI!

Koa from Aotearoa said

And Laura from Norway said

Pri from Sri Lanka said

HACH!

And Anja from Germany said

HATSCHI!

Plus, Jun next door said

HAKUSHON!

Max scratched his head.

Then he realised sneezes
must be like people —
the same but different.

Surely friends could be the
same but different too.

Max went home in search of his new neighbour Jun.

He spotted him outside his house. Jun grabbed the fluffy, fat feather and tickled Max's nose.

Max could feel a sneeze coming on. But instead of AH-CHOO, he decided to try and say HAKUSHON. Just like Jun.

Max took a great gulp of air.
'HAKU-CHOO!' he sneezed.

Jun giggled.
Max giggled too.

MAX
JUN
CLUBHOUSE
THIS WAY
UP

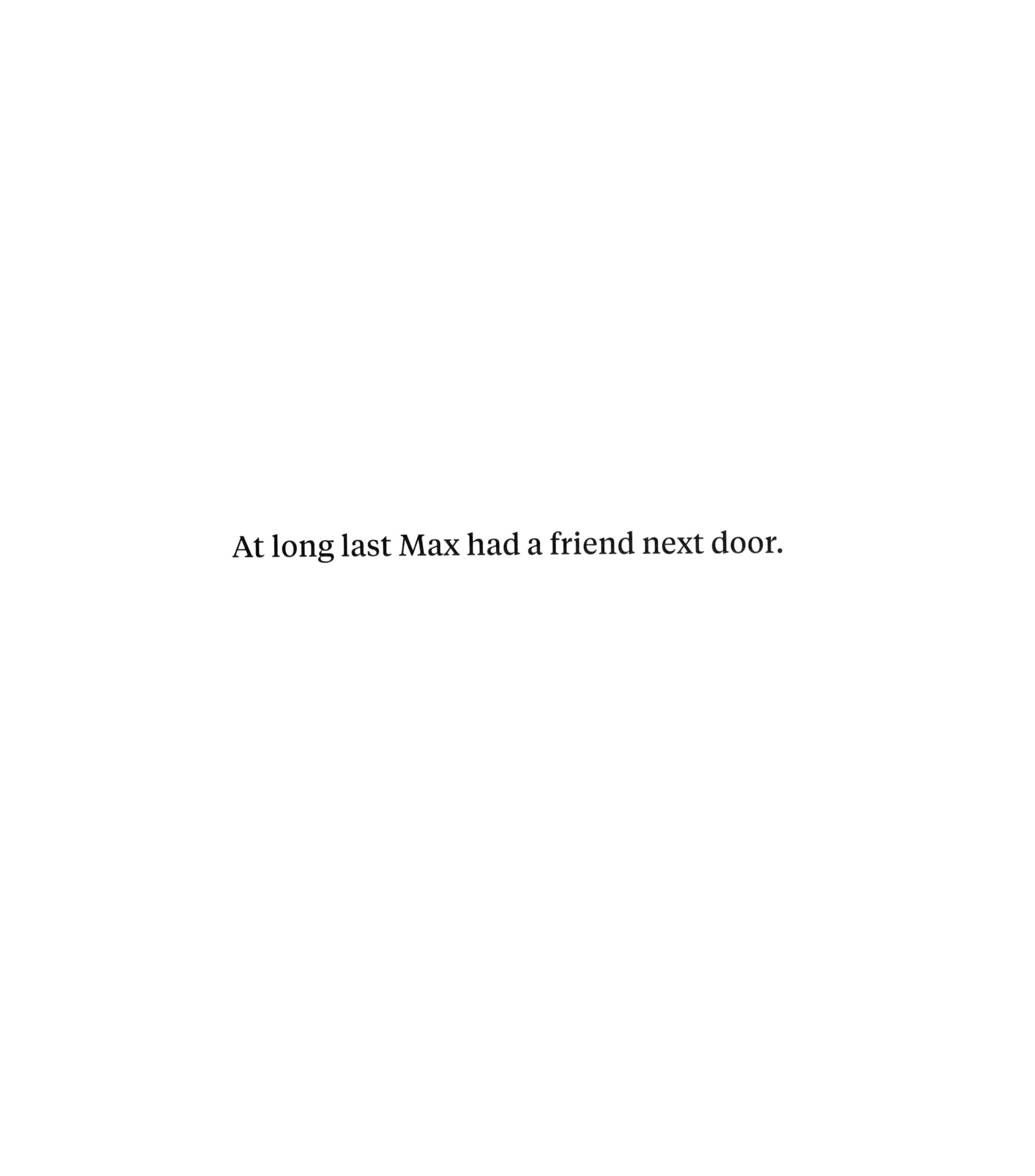

At long last Max had a friend next door.

And that was nothing to sneeze at.

Text © Angela Walker, 2023
Illustrations © Ross Hamilton, 2023

The moral rights of the authors have been asserted.

Typographical design © David Bateman Ltd, 2023

Published in 2023 by David Bateman Ltd,
Unit 2/5 Workspace Drive, Hobsonville,
Auckland 0618, New Zealand
www.batemanbooks.co.nz

ISBN: 978-1-77689-069-9

This book is copyright. Except for the purposes of fair review, no part may be stored or transmitted in any form or by any means, electronic or mechanical, including recording or storage in any information retrieval systems, without permission in writing from the publisher. No reproduction may be made, whether by photocopying or any other means, unless a licence has been obtained from the publisher or its agent.

A catalogue record for this book is available
from the National Library of New Zealand.

Book design: Spencer Levine
Printed in China by Toppan Leefung Printing Ltd